The Worry Glasses

Overcoming Anxiety

by

Donalisa Helsley

Illustrated by Kalpart

"Stress spares no one. Our children are deeply affected by it. One manifestation of stress in their lives is anxiety. Donalisa Helsley has written a wonderful story which will help children recognize how they are anxious and give them tools to help lessen the effects of anxiety in their lives. I highly recommend this book to both children and those who care for them." **John B. White, M.D., Board Certified Psychiatrist**

"The Worry Glasses identifies 'anxiety' in 'kid friendly' words giving them a vocabulary for their worries. Donalisa Helsley connects feelings with concrete behaviors so the child can understand how fears and worries are directly connected to how they behave or how they physically feel. It also educates parents on what anxiety looks like (from defiance to nightmares). I highly recommend this book to anyone working with or living with an anxious child. The book is straightforward and the exercises/techniques are easy for anyone (clinician, teacher or parent) to use." **Sarah Caliboso-Soto, Licensed Clinical Social Worker**

ISBN 978-1-61225-164-6

©Copyright 2012 Donalisa Helsley

Illustrations and Book Cover Design by Kalpart
Visit http://www.kalpart.com/

Published by Mirror Publishing
Milwaukee, WI 53214

Printed in the USA.

Pictured left to right: My daughters, Jadyn and Genesis, and Miss Jessica with their "worry glasses" and "worry box"

To the "real" MJ, Thanks for letting me use your beautiful red hair and name! You rock!

To my bestie, the "real" Miss Jessica, I love watching you work. Your passion and dedication to helping children shines. You are a super star. Now hurry up and get that Master's Degree. You can doooo it!

My name is Marjorie, but everyone calls me MJ. I love having fun, but I used to miss out on doing fun things because I was so worried. I didn't swim when my family went to Hawaii, because I was worried about sharks.

At camp, I didn't ride a horse because I was worried I might fall off and get hurt. I didn't go to my friend's party because I was worried no one would play with me.

Once I pretended to be sick for three whole days, because I was too scared to read my book report to the class. My stomach hurt, my hands were sweaty and tingly, and my heart beat very fast every time I thought about reading in front of the class. Sometimes I used to feel so dizzy that I couldn't stand and felt as if I couldn't breathe!

"MJ, what's wrong?" Mama said one day. "You don't play with your friends anymore. You are very quiet and look tired every morning before school."

"Mama, I feel so worried all the time. What if the kids at school laugh at me? What if they don't like me? Every night I toss and turn because I worry about all the bad things that might happen or go wrong the next day!"

7

"That's not good, MJ," Mama sympathized. "It sounds as if your brain is full of worries. I'm going to take you to the doctor to find out how to help you."

"Thanks, Mama. It doesn't feel good to worry all the time."

The next day, my parents and I went to a pediatrician. That's a kids' doctor. They decided I should talk to someone about my worries.

My mom took me to see a counselor. I was scared at first, but Miss Jessica, the counselor, was really nice. She played games and made crafts with me. She listened to me when I spoke to her. We talked about all my worries.

Scared

Anxiety

WORRY

Miss Jessica told me that it's normal to have some worries. "Everyone worries," she said. "Your parents, friends, teachers, and even I worry! When our minds are flooded with worries and fears that something bad will happen, it's called anxiety."

"So anxiety is another word for worry?"

"That's right. Anxiety is our body's response to stress and danger. Having some anxiety is normal and healthy; it can help warn us and get us out of dangerous situations."

"Miss Jessica," I said. "I can't sleep at night or think at school because so many worries are going through my mind."

"MJ, when anxiety occurs almost all the time and gets in the way of doing what a kid wants or needs to do, then it's not healthy. It's okay to be nervous about speaking in front of the class, but you shouldn't avoid it because of worry. Can you think of something you haven't done because of worry?"

"When I went to Hawaii, I didn't swim because I was scared of a shark attack."

"It was smart for you to know about sharks, but it's also important for you to know that your parents and the life guards would've protected you. When you are afraid of something you should try to learn more about it."

When we came home from Ms. Jessica's office, we looked up information about sharks together and found out they rarely attack humans. I wish I had known when I was in Hawaii! I'll know that for next time.

Together, Miss Jessica and I work on controlling my anxiety.

"MJ, anxiety is like magnifying glasses. I call them 'worry glasses.' When you have worry glasses on things look bigger and scarier than they really are."

"I've looked at tiny worms with a magnifying glass and it makes them look bigger. Is that what worry glasses are like?"

17

"Yes, you need to take off those worry glasses so you can see things like they really are. I'll teach you some coping skills to help you control your anxiety."

"Miss Jessica, what are coping skills?"

"Coping skills are things that you can do to help you deal with stressful situations or thoughts. Tell me something you enjoy doing."

"I like to dance and draw."

19

"Great, you already have two coping skills! Here is one I want you to do when you can't stop thinking something bad will happen. Take deep breaths and tell yourself 'I can do this.' Pretend you are a balloon.

"Fill your balloon with air deep from your belly, then slowly let the air out. Remember to let it out slowly so your body has a chance to calm down.

"Ok, let's practice. I'll be a green balloon. What color balloon are you?"

"I want to be a purple balloon!"

22

Miss Jessica and I did a fun activity where I thought about how "full" of worry I was. I could be full "up to my knees" — a little worried, "up to my stomach" — really worried, and "up to my head" —want to hide worried.

When I am worried about something now, I talk to my parents and I decide how full of worry I am. Talking about my fears helps! When I talk about them, my fears become less powerful.

My mom cuts out paper in the shape of glasses and I write my worries on them. She puts them away in my Worry Box that I decorated.

24

Later, I talk about my worries with my parents, an adult I trust, or Miss Jessica. I still worry sometimes at school or feel afraid of something.

It's okay because it's normal to have some worries. I just don't let the worries keep me from doing what I need and want to do. When my worries start to get out of control my parents remind me to take off my worry glasses and see the problem in the right size.

I know that I have the power and I am in control of my anxiety.

Anxiety is not the boss of me.
I am the boss of my anxiety!

Anxiety Relieving Exercises

Here are some fun anxiety-relieving exercises I do with my friends. They really like them. I hope you do too!

Balloon Breath

Imagine you are blowing up a balloon. Take in a deep breath, and slowly blow up your balloon. See the balloon getting bigger and bigger and bigger. Now close your eyes and imagine the balloon floating into the air. As you stand there, feel yourself becoming very quiet and peaceful. Repeat this exercise 2 or 3 times. When you are feeling worried, you can blow up the balloon, fill it with worry thoughts, put it on the floor and stomp on it.

The Worry Box

Decorate a shoe box anyway you want to. Then cut up paper in strips or in the shape of glasses. On those pieces of paper you write down your worries. Then put them in the box so that you

can focus on what you need or want to do. Later with an adult you can visit your worry box and talk about the worries with someone you trust.

How Full of Worry Are You?

Practice figuring out how full of worry you are. "Up to my knees" a little worried - you can put this worry aside and talk to someone about it later. "Up to my stomach" really worried - talk to someone about it as soon as possible. "Up to my head" want to hide worried - STOP! Talk to someone right NOW!

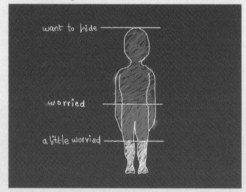

Magical Thumb

Whenever you are feeling stressed or anxious hold your left hand with your right hand, placing your right thumb in the middle of your left palm. Gently stroke your thumb in a circle around your palm. This should help you relax.

Parent Tips

If you have concerns or questions about possible symptoms of anxiety in your child, be sure to talk with your pediatrician. Sometimes, it is tricky to identify anxiety in children. Your child might find it difficult to express their anxiety so they hide it or their anxiety exhibits as a defiant behaviors and temper tantrums.

Here are some signs of anxiety in children:
- Anger, aggression, restlessness, irritability, tantrums, opposition and defiance
- Worrying constantly about things that might happen or have happened
- Physical complaints such as stomach aches, headaches, fatigue, etc.
- Avoiding or refusing to do things or go places
- Having difficulty falling or staying asleep, nightmares, or night terrors
- Extreme clinginess and separation anxiety
- Withdrawal from social interactions and activities
- Constantly imagining the worst, over-exaggerating the negatives, self-criticism

What to do to help your child that is struggling with anxiety:

- Exercise can relieve stress and help your child relax.
- Establish consistent daily routines. The predictability helps reduce anxiety.
- Help your child identify what they are feeling and talk about their feelings. At first it will be difficult for them so watch and listen carefully for the times when your child expresses feelings indirectly through behaviors. Verbalize it for them.
- Respect your child's fears. Resist the urge to tell them to stop being afraid or to minimize their feelings. Acknowledge their fears and let them know that you will help them overcome these fears.
- Teach and practice relaxation skills. This will help them feel better when they are anxious, worried or scared. Learning to control their body will help them realize that they are in control of anxiety.

My Warp Speed Mind
coming soon!

CPSIA information can be obtained at www.ICGtesting.com
Printed in the USA
BVIW12n0918110615
404000BV00010B/106